DENNIS the MENACE

A MONSTER MENACE!

BEANO books

published under licence by

meadowside
CHILDREN'S BOOKS

SCHOOL TRIP

Dennis was going on a school trip.

Mum and Dad were very nervous.

The headmaster was extremely nervous.

The other teachers were just very glad they weren't going on the trip.

The only teacher who wasn't nervous was Mr Glossop. He was new, and he didn't know about Dennis yet. People had tried to warn him, but he just laughed and shook his head at them.

"Every child should be allowed to go on school trips!" he said. "It's educational!"

"It's insane," said the headmaster. He had only ever allowed Dennis to go on one school trip in all his years at

Beanotown School.

Once was enough. The teacher in charge was still undergoing therapy!

On the morning of the trip, Mum checked Dennis's school bag and all his pockets for menacing equipment. But his pockets were empty and there was nothing in his bag except pencils, a notebook and a packed lunch.

"Oh Dennis," said Mum happily. "I'm so proud of you! You have decided to be good on your school trip!"

"Yeah," agreed Dennis as Mum waved him goodbye from the front door. "I'm gonna be very good... at menacing!"

Dennis waited until Mum had gone inside, then dived into the garden hedge and pulled out his best menacing gear.

"Lucky I thought to stash this here last night!" he grinned as he stuffed his catapult, water pistol, stink bombs and peashooter into his pockets. Then he raced to school where the bus was waiting. Most of the class were already on board. Pie Face and Curly were on the back seat. Curly was pinging elastic bands at Bertie Blenkinsop. Pie Face was munching on his first packed lunch already. Everyone's mouths fell open when they saw Dennis.

"Siiirrr!" whined Walter the Softy. "Sir, Dennis is trying to sneak onto the bus, sir!"

"That's quite all right, Walter," smiled Mr Glossop. "Dennis is coming too."

4

Walter went white as Curly gave a loud cheer.

"Brilliant! This is gonna be the best school trip ever!"

Dennis elbowed his way to the back of the bus and squashed in next to his friends. Mr Glossop stood up at the front of the bus.

"Quiet, everyone! We have a very exciting day in front of us! We are going to the Beanotown Museum."

Walter, Bertie and Spotty were bouncing up and down with excitement.

"Will there be long lectures about the past?" asked Walter eagerly.

"Are you going to set us a test after the visit?" Bertie said hopefully.

"YOWEEE!" said Spotty.

"What is the meaning of that?" asked Mr Glossop. "Quiet, boy!"

"Somebody fired something at the back of my head!" Spotty wailed. Mr Glossop glanced up the bus, but no one was holding a peashooter or a catapult.

"I expect it was Dennis!" sneaked Walter.

"Well?" asked Mr Glossop, looking at Dennis, who had just slipped his catapult behind his back.

"Who sir, me sir?" said Dennis with a shrug. Mr Glossop frowned at Spotty.

"Stop crying, boy, it must have been a fly. Now, pay attention everyone. There are two exciting exhibitions at the Beanotown Museum. First we will be finding out all about dinosaurs. Then we will learn about ancient Egypt. I want you all on your best behaviour, is that clear?"

"Yes Mr Glossop!" chanted the softies.

"Our best menacing behaviour!" chuckled Dennis.

When they arrived, the Curator was standing on the Museum steps to meet them.

"Good morning, children," he said. "How are we all today?"

"Humph, he's talking to us as if we're babies!" grumbled Dennis.

"Follow me into the Hall of Dinosaurs!" beamed the Curator. "Isn't this exciting, children?"

"Ooh, *yes!*" exclaimed Walter. "I hope that none of the dinosaurs are too scary!"

"I'll make sure you don't see anything that will frighten you!" said the Curator. "Just don't look up as we go through the first hall!"

He led them through the Hall of Dinosaurs, past life-size models of Triceratops, Pterodactyls and Velociraptors. Walter, Bertie and Spotty looked down at the ground so they wouldn't get scared.

"I don't want to have nightmares!" said Bertie.

"Brilliant!" said Dennis, looking up at the giant models. "Dinosaurs are the all-time best menaces ever... apart from me!"

But the Curator didn't stop next to the models. He took them into a smaller room that was full of small rocks in glass cases.

He stopped in front of a tiny table. The class gathered around with the softies at the front.

"What is it?" asked Dennis.

"I can't see," said Pie Face, squinting through the crowd. "Are there any fossilised pies?"

"This is very exciting indeed," said the Curator. "It is an amber fossil with a tiny insect trapped inside!"

The softies gasped and Dennis gave a loud groan. "Never mind the fossils, what about the dinosaurs?" he asked.

"Aha, well I think you'll find this next exhibit very thrilling," said the Curator. He led them over to where a small skeleton was on display.

"This was an animal called Eohippus," he said.

"Did it have lots of fights?" asked Curly hopefully.

"No, it was a sweet little animal," said the Curator.

"What did it do when it was attacked, then?" asked Minnie.

"It ran away very fast," the Curator replied.

"Bor-ing," groaned Pie Face.

Dennis looked around at his classmates. Apart from the softies, they were all yawning.

"I don't like dinosaurs," said Curly.

"Come with me," whispered Dennis. "Dinosaurs are awesome –

and I'm gonna show you what they were really like!"

Dennis, Curly and Pie Face crept out of the fossil room and back into the Hall of Dinosaurs. A few of their classmates saw them going and followed them. Meanwhile, Dennis shinned up the leg of a scaly Triceratops and stood on its back.

"Triceratops was one of the most savage fighters ever!" he told Curly and Pie Face. "It used to run at its enemies with its horns down like this!"

Dennis kicked the model forward and jumped off it. The Triceratops toppled forward and crashed to the floor, trapping Minnie between its three horns!

"YOWCH! GET ME OUTTA HERE!"

Minnie hollered. Curly, Pie Face and Dennis roared with laughter.

"Minnie's been captured by a prehistoric menace!" chortled Curly as Dennis climbed up one of the ropes that supported the T-Rex model.

"The T-Rex was the all-time greatest dinosaur!" he bawled down to his classmates on the ground. "Its teeth were like knife blades and it was bigger than a double-decker bus!"

13

But suddenly the model started to sway. The rope that Dennis had used to climb up had been loosened and the model began to rock from side to side. There was a scream from one of the museum visitors.

"EEEEK!

The dinosaurs are coming to life! The T-Rex is walking!"

There was pandemonium as the visitors raced for the exits. The Curator rushed into the Hall of Dinosaurs, followed by Mr Glossop and the softies.

"Come back!" the Curator called to the visitors.

"They're alive!" squeaked Walter, fainting on the spot. Spotty and Bertie caught him and carried him back into the fossil room, fanning him with a homework book.

"Good heavens!" cried Mr Glossop, as the T-Rex tipped to one side and Dennis slid down its tail to the ground.

"Will SOMEONE get me outta here?" bellowed Minnie.

Mr Glossop glanced at the Curator, who was going an interesting shade of green.

"Er, I think it's about time for something to eat!" he said quickly. "Everybody outside to the park!"

Dennis, Curly and Pie Face raced out to the park in front of the museum. The grass was littered with people in various states of shock. A reporter from the Beanotown Gazette was walking around trying to get interviews. Dennis grinned as he opened his bag and pulled out his packed lunch.

"Excellent menacing," he said, chomping on a sausage-and-mustard sandwich.

"Here come the softies," said Curly, pointing as Walter tottered out and collapsed onto the grass.

"Would you like something to eat, Walter?" asked Spotty.

"Oh yes, a lettuce leaf please!" gasped Walter. "What a terrible shock!"

"I'll get you back for that!" Minnie shouted to Dennis. She wasn't looking forward to telling her mum how she got three holes in her new jumper.

"So, do you still think dinosaurs are boring?" Dennis asked Pie Face and Curly.

"Dinosaurs are wicked!" said Pie Face as he opened his third packed lunch.

"Yeah, I wish we didn't have to go to the stupid Egyptian exhibition later," added Curly.

Before Dennis could reply, Mr Glossop walked over to him.

"I've had a talk with the Curator, Dennis. I have managed to persuade him that it was all a terrible misunderstanding."

"Yeah," chortled Dennis under his breath. "He misunderstood that we aren't all softies!"

"He is willing to give you another chance. So you can come to the Egyptian exhibition with the rest of the class."

Mr Glossop went off to check on Walter and Dennis grinned at his friends.

"We'll have to see just how menacing the ancient Egyptians really were!" he chuckled.

Back inside the Museum, the Curator took the class into the Hall of Egypt.

"Welcome back to the Museum, dear children," he said in a sugary voice. "This is the Hall of Egypt, and soon you will get the chance to go inside a model of a pyramid.

19

You mustn't go very far inside because I don't want you little ones to get lost. Just a few steps will be enough. Now, first a little bit of history. Back in ancient Egypt..."

"Blah blah blah," sighed Pie Face as his stomach gave a loud gurgle. "Is it time for my teatime pie yet?"

But Dennis had spotted the entrance to the model pyramid.

"Come on!" he said. "Let's skip the boring history part and do some hands-on learning!"

They crept over to the entrance and slipped inside. They found themselves in a long tunnel. Candlelight glimmered and made

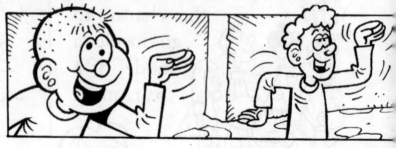

their shadows huge. Dennis struck a pose.

"This is how the Egyptians used to walk!" he chortled. "Too slow for menacing, though!"

They raced down the corridor and soon came to a place where two paths crossed.

"Let's split up!" grinned Dennis. "Last one to the centre of the pyramid is a softy!"

Dennis dashed off and thundered through the twisting paths of the pyramid. He was going at such a high speed that he didn't realise he'd reached the centre until it was too late!

CRASH!

He cannoned into the display in the middle of the pyramid. He and the display smashed to the floor. Dennis sprang to his feet and a huge grin spread over his face. He had knocked a mummy case to the ground and the lid had fallen off! Inside the case was what looked like a huge pile of bandages.

"Aha!" cried Dennis. "Just what I need to get me outta here!"

He tied one end of the bandages to the mummy case. Then he took the other end and started to walk back the way he had come. Every time he took a wrong turn, the bandage showed him where he had come from. All he had to do was roll it back into his arms.

Meanwhile, no one had noticed

that the menaces were missing. Half the class was asleep after the Curator's long history lesson. Even Mr Glossop felt his head nodding.

"Right, now for a look inside the model pyramid!" said the Curator. Mr Glossop's head shot up and he rubbed his eyes.

"Fascinating, fascinating," he said. "Come on, class, into the pyramid!"

"Remember, don't go too far!" called the Curator.

Walter wanted to stay outside – it all looked a bit too scary. But the class streamed into the pyramid and Walter was carried along with them.

"Help! Help!" he cried as he was swept into the dark corridor. He pressed himself against one of the walls until all his classmates had gone.

It was suddenly very quiet. Walter wondered where Spotty and Bertie were. Then, suddenly, a terrifying creature appeared in the candlelight. It was covered in bandages from head to foot, walking stiffly and slowly.

"A MUMMY!" Walter cried. "Oh Mumsy!"

And he fainted for the second time that day. Dennis heard the thump as Walter hit the floor and peered around his armfuls of bandages. He had taken the wrong turn quite often, and he had used a lot of the bandage.

"What are you doing down there,

you softy?" asked Dennis. Then he realised what had happened and chortled.

"Top menace! Hmm, maybe I can fool Curly and Pie Face too!"

Dennis could see the exit now. He quickly wrapped himself up in the bandage, leaving one end trailing behind him.

"Har har!" he thought. "Curly and Pie Face are gonna jump outta their skins when they see me! They'll never think Egypt is boring after this!"

Dennis stalked out of the pyramid with his arms held out in front of him, just as the Curator was talking to the head of the Beanotown Egyptian Society. She saw Dennis and screamed.

"It's a mummy! Run!"

Dennis followed her as she ran out of the hall. Her screams terrified the other visitors, who were still feeling shaky about the dinosaur incident that morning. When they saw Dennis in his bandages, they went berserk.

The Museum was in chaos! Half the visitors fainted and the other half was crammed into the massive doorway, trying to be the first to escape.

Suddenly the Curator clapped his hands to his head. "I know that bandage! He gasped. "I recognise that bandage!" He raced into the pyramid and found the smashed display.

"Our ancient mummy!" he wailed. "It can never be replaced!"

Mr Glossop led everyone out of

the pyramid. When he noticed that Dennis was missing, his eyes narrowed. His jaws clenched. He imagined the headmaster saying, "I told you so," in his smuggest voice.

"**DENNIS!**" he bellowed.

As visitors were carried out on stretchers and the hysterical Curator was led away by a trained nurse, Mr Glossop spotted the end of a white bandage sticking out from behind a bush in the park. He picked it up and followed it behind the bush, where Dennis, Curly and Pie Face were sharing Pie Face's fourth packed lunch and chortling. Mr Glossop yanked on the bandage and pulled Dennis to his feet.

29

"Sir, I was only trying to show Curly and Pie Face how interesting ancient Egypt can be!" Dennis grinned.

"Well, I've got something interesting to show you!" said Mr Glossop. He marched Dennis back to the Museum and into the natural history section. He stopped in front of a huge skeleton display.

"Do you know what this is?" asked Mr Glossop.

"The skeleton of a whale," said Dennis, looking at the label.

"It's also where you're going to spend the rest of the day!" roared Mr Glossop.

Dennis tried to struggle but Mr Glossop just tightened the bandages. Before he could think of a way to escape, Dennis was trapped inside the whale skeleton.

"**GRRR!**" he fumed. "**Let me go!**"

"This way the class can enjoy the rest of their visit in peace!" said Mr Glossop, walking away. "And the visitors can enjoy a brand new dinosaur – the Menacesaurus!"

THE GREAT SAUSAGE QUEST

Dennis was not planning to do any menacing at all today.

He was far too busy.

Today was Gnasher's birthday and Dennis was planning a big surprise party for him. There had been a lot to organise. Dennis had arranged almost everything, but there was one very important thing left.

He left Gnasher chasing cats around the garden (just for practice) and jumped on his skateboard.

Dennis whizzed down the street, trying out a few of his latest moves as he went. When he arrived outside the butcher's shop, he back-kicked his board under his arm and strolled in.

"And what can I do for you?" asked the butcher cheerfully. (He was one of the very few people in Beanotown who were always glad to see Dennis.)

"Sausages," said Dennis. "Lots and lots of sausages."

The butcher shook his head.

"I'm sorry, Dennis," he said. "We've had a run on sausages this morning and my fresh delivery hasn't arrived. I don't have any sausages left!"

Dennis gaped at the butcher.

"But Gnasher's gotta have sausages for his birthday!" he groaned. "There must be somewhere I can get some?"

"Well," said the butcher thoughtfully. "The lifeguard at the swimming pool bought a lot of sausages here this morning. He's organising the annual party for the Synchronised Swimming Club. Perhaps he could spare some?"

"Only softies do synchronised swimming," said Dennis, "and they don't even like sausages. I'll buy them off the lifeguard!"

Dennis ran out of the shop, jumped on his board and headed for the swimming pool. But when he walked in, the receptionist held out a hand.

"Ticket please," she said.

"I don't have a ticket," said Dennis. "I just—"

"Are you part of the synchronised swimming team?" she asked.

"NO!" roared Dennis in disgust. "I only want to speak to—"

"No ticket, no entry," snapped the receptionist.

Fuming, Dennis bought a ticket and stomped into the changing room. Bertie Blenkinsop was just pulling on a pair of lemon-yellow swimming trunks. He glared at Dennis.

"Riff-raff like you can't be in here while we're practising our routine," he said.

"I've got a ticket," Dennis replied.

"Ticket or no ticket, you can't go into the swimming area dressed like that!" sniffed Bertie. He walked out of the changing room and Dennis g l a n c e d around. There was a spare pair of s w i m m i n g trunks hanging on a peg. Dennis quickly swiped them, changed and headed out to the pool.

The water was filled with softies working on a synchronised swimming routine. Walter was in the middle, wearing his orange water wings. The sides of the pool were crowded with even more softies, waiting for their turn. Dennis could see the lifeguard on the other side of the pool, but he couldn't reach him through the throngs of softies.

"'Scuse me, mister!" Dennis called across the pool. But the lifeguard was showing Spotty Perkins how to put his goggles on and he didn't hear anything.

"OY!" bellowed Dennis. The lifeguard still didn't react.

"Right," said Dennis. "There's only one thing for it!"

He stepped back, sucked in a deep breath and then took a running jump into the crowded pool. As Dennis dive bombed into the water, he created a tidal wave that splashed four softies out of the pool.

"EEEK!" squealed Walter as he lost one of his water wings. "Help! I can't swim without my water wings!"

The lifeguard dived into the pool and rescued Walter. Then he tried to calm down the trembling softies. Dennis heaved himself out of the water and dripped over to the lifeguard.

"Excuse me," he said. "Did you buy loads of sausages from the butcher this morning?"

"Yes I did," snapped the lifeguard. "So what?"

"It's Gnasher's birthday today and the butcher has run out of sausages," explained Dennis. "I thought you could sell me some of yours, seeing as these softies don't like sausages anyway!"

"Look at my swimming pool!" roared the lifeguard. "Look at the synchronised swimming team! It'll be weeks before I can get them back in the water now! I can't spare sausages for a menace like you! Clear off!"

Dennis was furious, but the lifeguard had made up his mind. He stomped back to the changing room, put his clothes on and headed back to see the butcher.

When Dennis walked back into the shop, the butcher shook his head.

"Sorry," he said. "The delivery still hasn't arrived."

"Where am I going to find enough sausages now?" Dennis groaned. "Gnasher's birthday is gonna be ruined!"

"Maybe Miss Bugg could help you out," suggested the butcher. "She bought lots of sausages for her cats this morning."

"CATS!" exclaimed Dennis. "A bunch of cats don't need all those sausages!"

He jumped back on his skateboard and whizzed up the road towards Miss Bugg's house. He was thinking so hard about finding some sausages for Gnasher, he didn't even notice Curly and Pie Face waving at him

from across the street. Dennis jumped off his board outside Miss Bugg's house. It wasn't the kind of house that Dennis went near if he could help it. There were pink frilly curtains in every window. The walls of the house were salmon pink, and someone had painted cats' faces all around the door. The bushes had been trimmed so they looked like giant green cats and there were cat-shaped wind chimes hanging from every tree and tinkling.

"What a place!" muttered Dennis to himself. "But it's for Gnasher, so I have to go in!"

He pushed open the gate and stepped into the garden.

"YUCK!" growled Dennis. "CATS!"

The garden was swarming with

cats of every colour, size and breed. Big cats, small cats, fat cats and thin cats were all crammed into the tiny garden. Some of them were asleep, some were washing themselves, some were chasing mice and some were chasing each other. But, as soon as Dennis walked into the garden, every single one of them stopped what they were doing and stared at him.

One by one, the cats started to sniff. This boy definitely smelled strange. SNIFF! Stink bombs. SNIFF! Sausage sandwiches. The cats got a little closer. Then a breeze moved Dennis's trouser legs and released a smell that filled the cats with terror.

DOG!

And not just any dog – they could smell GNASHER!

The cats went wild. They had to get away from that terrible smell! There was a frenzy of yowls, teeth and claws as they all tried to escape.

SPLASH! Two white Persians made a leap for the water butt before they realised that the lid wasn't on.

MeeYOWK! Three ginger toms tried to crawl through a hole in the fence at the same time and got wedged in place. One small black-and-white cat scrabbled through the letterbox and got stuck halfway, while there was a pile-up at the cat flap. Several highly strung Siamese decided to climb up the side of the house and got tangled in the ivy, and a tortoiseshell kitten shot up the willow tree and sat on the highest branch, trembling. The rest of the cats raced around the garden in circles, searching for a way out with their fur sticking on end.

"Mental," said Dennis, shaking his head and staring at the pandemonium. "Who'd have a cat?"

Just then the front door opened and Miss Bugg peered out over her pince-nez. When she saw her cats her hands flew to her mouth.

"Oh my poor darlings! Oh my sweet pussycats!" Then she saw Dennis standing in the middle of the garden path. "What have you done to them, you horrid nasty boy?"

"Nothing!" exclaimed Dennis.

"They're bonkers! Anyway, never mind about them! It's my dog Gnasher's birthday today and I don't have any sausages for him. Will you sell me some of yours? Your cats don't need them as much as I do!"

"Gnasher?" shrieked Miss Bugg, pulling the cat out of the letterbox. "A dog? Get out of here. Go on – shoo! You've done something to my cats and I'm not selling sausages to such a naughty menace!"

She slammed the door and Dennis frowned.

"Crazy cats!" he fumed. **"NOW** where am I going to find Gnasher's birthday sausages?"

Dennis sped back to the shop again, hoping that the delivery had arrived. But the butcher just shrugged his shoulders.

"Sorry, Dennis, the delivery man has just called in. His lorry has broken down!"

"Oh no!" Dennis groaned. "Miss Bugg won't let me buy her sausages because of her mental mangy moggies. What am I gonna do now?"

"Well, I sold the rest of my sausages to Sergeant Slipper," said the butcher. "But I didn't think you'd want to ask him!"

"Anything for Gnasher's birthday!" Dennis sighed. He tucked his skateboard under his arm and scooted to the police station. But before he could ring the bell, he spotted something lying on the ground outside the front door. It was a new, shiny pound coin!

"Hmm," said Dennis thoughtfully. "I wonder..."

He knelt down beside the pound and, as he expected, it jerked away. Dennis narrowed his eyes.

"So, someone thinks they can menace the Menace, do they?" he said. "We'll see about that!"

His menacing vision helped him spot the almost-invisible wire. He was concentrating so hard on working out where it was coming from, he didn't notice the door of the police station opening. He didn't see Sergeant Slipper come striding down the path. And Sergeant Slipper didn't see Dennis, kneeling on the ground, until it was too late.

"ARRGGHH!" yelled Sergeant Slipper as he tripped over Dennis and hurtled through the air.

"YOWEEEE!" he bellowed as he shot headfirst into the hedge.

Dennis couldn't hold back a snort of laughter. Sergeant Slipper pulled himself out of the hedge, his hair full of twigs.

"You little menace!" he roared.

"Maybe you should look where you're going next time!" Dennis chuckled. "Listen, it's Gnasher's birthday today and the butcher has run out of sausages. I thought maybe I could buy some of yours?"

Sergeant Slipper's face went from pink to yellow to red, and finally to glowing purple. His eyes bulged. He opened and closed his mouth, but no sound came out. He started to walk towards Dennis, who realised that it was time to go. He jumped on his skateboard.

"Yeah, well, it was worth a try!" he grinned, and whizzed off before the Sergeant could grab him.

Dennis felt terrible as he made his way home. He had plenty of ice cream and boxes full of cakes for Gnasher's surprise party, as well as a first-class juicy bone. But he knew that Gnasher would be really disappointed when he found out that there were no sausages.

"This is a menacing disaster," Dennis thought as he walked in to the kitchen. Then he stopped. He could hear a loud noise coming from the sitting room and there was a very familiar smell in the air. Dennis raced to the sitting room and stopped in astonishment. The room was all ready for Gnasher's party, with balloons and streamers in every corner and plates of food on every surface. There was a crowd of people in the room, but best of all there were hundreds and hundreds of...

"SAUSAGES!"

yelled Dennis, punching the air. There were sausages on sticks and sausages on their own. There were sausages of every size and type. Best of all, Curly and Pie Face had made a huge Dennis-shaped display entirely out of sausages.

"Wicked!" grinned Dennis. "But where did they all come from?"

"We've had a lot of visitors this afternoon!" said Mum, dangling a string of sausages from the lampshade in the corner. Dennis saw the butcher unpacking another box of sausages.

"The delivery arrived just in time!" he told Dennis.

A heavy hand clapped Dennis on the back. It was the lifeguard from the swimming pool.

"Decided I'd been a bit unfair!" he boomed. "Anyway, I didn't realise that all the softies are vegetarian! So I've brought half my sausages along for Gnasher!"

"Brilliant, thanks!" grinned Dennis.

"And I changed my mind too," twittered Miss Bugg. "Gnasher keeps my darling cats healthy by giving them so much exercise all year long. So he can have half of my sausages too!"

"Awesome!" Dennis chuckled. He looked around at the room. There were plenty of plates of food and loads of sausages. Curly and Pie Face and all his most menacing friends were there to help him celebrate. There was only one thing left to do – fetch the birthday dog!

Dennis blindfolded Gnasher and led him into the sitting room. Then he undid the blindfold.

"SURPRISE!" shouted all the guests.

"GNASH!" barked Gnasher in amazement. His jaws fell open when he saw all the sausages!

"Happy birthday, mate!" Dennis chortled. "Tuck in!"

The party was a huge success, and Gnasher took great pleasure in biting lumps out of Dennis... the sausage version, that is!

THE HOUND OF THE MENACES

It had been a long, soggy and annoying day.

That morning, Dad had decided that what the whole family needed was a long walk in the countryside. He had ignored Bea's wails, grabbed Dennis before he could do a runner and driven them all out to the Beanotown moors. It was too far to walk back and Dad had locked the car, so Dennis had no choice. He pulled on his wellies, hunched up his shoulders and stomped off after Mum, Dad and Bea.

First it had rained.

Then it had hailed.

Then it had rained and hailed at the same time.

"I am NOT HAPPY!" Dennis had growled, trudging along behind Mum and Dad.

"GNESH," agreed Gnasher.

61

"This will build character!" said Dad.

"I've GOT character," grumbled Dennis.

"Come on!" said Mum cheerfully, as rain streamed down the back of her neck. "Just two more miles and we'll stop for a nice spam sandwich!"

"What's wrong with a dry house, a bag of sweets and a comic?" Dennis groaned.

"Fresh air is good for you!" bellowed Dad.

"It might be good for parents," said Dennis, "but it's definitely not good for menaces!"

When they had finally got back to the car, it was starting to get dark and they were all soaking wet. Dad refused to look at the map because he said he knew the way home. After about ten minutes they were completely lost.

"We should have turned left at that signpost!" fumed Mum.

"We did!" Dad exclaimed.

"Well we should have turned right, then!" argued Mum.

On the back seat, Dennis was giving Bea a few quick menacing lessons and sharing a bag of glow-in-the-dark sweets with Gnasher. He fired a lemon drop at Bea with his peashooter and she dodged it expertly.

"You're getting pretty good!" said Dennis, impressed, as the lemon drop shot into Dad's left ear. The Menace grinned and Bea giggled as his luminous teeth shone.

"These glow-in-the-dark sweets are awesome," Dennis chuckled.

"Perhaps we should stop and ask for directions?" suggested Mum as she pulled the lemon drop out of Dad's ear with a loud POP! "We just passed an old hostel – they should be able to help."

Suddenly there was a worrying sort of KERDUNK from the car's engine. The car began to shudder and slow down. Then the engine stalled completely and the car rolled to a standstill.

Dad's knuckles went white as he gripped the steering wheel.

"Broke down! Broke down!" Bea sang, whacking the back of Dad's head with her rattle.

"There's a phone box just up there," said Dad. "I'll go and call the repair services."

Dad clambered out of the car and Mum watched him make the call. She saw him go purple in the face. She saw him waving his arms around and shaking his fist at the receiver. Then he slammed it down and strode back to the car. His left eye was twitching, which was a bad sign. He got back into the car and glared at Dennis.

"The emergency services aren't coming," he said. "They've got a very big file on this family. The man I spoke to asked if Dennis was with us. When I said he was, do you know what he said?"

"What?" asked Mum.

"NOTHING!" bawled Dad. **"HE HUNG UP!"**

"Excellent menacing result!" chortled Dennis.

"So, to sum up," said Mum, who had been looking forward to a nice cup of tea when she got home. "We've broken down on a stormy night in the middle of the moor and no one is coming to rescue us."

"We'll just have to push the car home," said Dad.

"Oho no!" said Mum. For a

moment she looked just like Dennis. Dad's knees trembled. "We are going back to that hostel and getting beds for the night. In the morning you can call a local garage to fix the car. But I am not pushing the car all the way back to Beanotown, and that's final!"

Ten minutes later they were dripping rainwater all over the entrance hall of the crumbling old hostel. There was no one in sight, but there was a large bell on the reception desk. Dennis picked it up and rang it.

CLANG!

Immediately a door opened behind the reception desk and a man peered out at them. He had a long, curving nose and jet-black hair slicked back with greasy gel.

"It's Count Dracula!" chortled Dennis to Gnasher.

"I'm Mr Mulch, the owner," said the man. "What do you want?"

Mum explained what had happened.

"All the rooms are taken," snapped Mr Mulch. "You can't stay here."

"There must be somewhere we could sleep!" Mum exclaimed. At that moment the door opened again and a woman stepped out. She had narrow eyes and long black ringlets that coiled around her face like snakes.

"This is my wife," said Mr Mulch. "My dear, these people want a room for the night."

"The only space is out in the garden," said Mrs Mulch hoarsely. "There are a couple of tents out there. But it will be a cold, stormy night. It would be better if you found somewhere else."

"Oh, er, well perhaps we should go..." stammered Mum.

"No way, this place is cool!" Dennis exclaimed, looking around at the cobwebby old building. "I wonder if it's haunted!"

"The garden will be fine," said Dad, glaring at Dennis.

"You've missed dinner," said Mr Mulch. "We can't feed you."

"That's all right," said Mum. "I've got plenty of spam sandwiches left over."

Bea curled her lip.

"I'm not sure we should let you stay out in the garden," said Mr Mulch. "It's on just such a night as this that the Hound of the Moor walks!"

"Pardon?" gulped Dad.

"The Hound of the Moor!" hissed Mrs Mulch. "A terrible red beast that stalks the moor on stormy nights, searching for prey!"

70

"Wicked!" said Dennis.

"Oo-er," said Mum.

"Its howls make your blood run cold," Mrs Mulch continued. "And its luminous jaws shine in the moonlight."

"They say that if you see its jaws, it will carry you off and you will never be seen again!" added Mr Mulch.

There was a long silence.

"I'd like to meet it," said Dennis.

"Me too!" smiled Bea. "Nice doggy!"

"The tents will be fine," said Mum. "We'll take them."

Mr Mulch looked as if he wanted to argue, but he just took the money and handed them a torch.

"I'll show you the way," he snapped. "Follow me."

He led them through long, echoing corridors, with polished wooden floors and expensive-looking rugs.

"These would make awesome slides!" grinned Dennis. He backed up, ran towards the rug and then skidded down the corridor. **"GANGWAY!"** yelled Dennis, but Mr Mulch was too slow. Dennis crashed into him and they somersaulted into a table. The vase that was on the table shot into the air, smashed against the ceiling and showered everyone in tiny pieces of porcelain.

"You little menace!" shouted Mr Mulch, shaking the pieces of vase out of his greasy hair.

"Er, let's get out to the tents," said Dad, before Mr Mulch could say anything about chequebooks.

The hostel owner led them to the back door and turned a large key. The door swung open with a loud CREEAKK. Dad switched on the torch and they saw two tents in the garden.

"There are sleeping bags inside," said Mr Mulch. "Remember, if you hear the hound howling, don't step out of the tents! And whatever you do, don't go over to that part of the garden."

He pointed over to where a stone wall separated a small area of the garden.

"Wh... why not?" asked Dad.

"Because that's where we have found the hound's paw prints!" hissed Mr Mulch.

"Brilliant!" said Dennis. Mr Mulch glared at him.

"That part of the garden is out of

bounds!" he said. "No menaces allowed!"

He pushed them out into the garden and slammed the door shut behind them. They heard the big key scrape as he turned it in the lock.

"Right, come on Gnasher!" said Dennis, heading for the stone wall. But a hand gripped the back of his neck.

"Oh no you don't," said Dad. "You heard what Mr Mulch said. You're not allowed over there, so get into your tent and go to sleep!"

"No way!" said Dennis. "Mr Mulch is hiding something and I wanna know what it is!"

"Buried treasure!" Bea gurgled.

"Rubbish!" Dad replied. "It's very kind of them to let us stay when they have no rooms free!"

"It is funny though," said Mum.

"This place is very well furnished for a hostel. Did you notice those expensive rugs? And that vase must have cost a fortune!"

"Shhh!" said Dad, thinking of his chequebook again. "Let's just go to sleep!"

Mum and Dad took Bea into one tent with them, while Dennis and Gnasher shared the other. There were no lights on in the hostel and the only sound came from the canvas of the tent shaking in the wind. Soon Dad's snores were rumbling around the garden. Dennis sat up and grinned at Gnasher.

"Come on!" he said. "I bet Bea's right! The Mulches have probably got stacks of treasure buried in this garden. Let's go hunting!"

They crept out of the tent and Dennis headed for the stone wall, but suddenly Gnasher stopped and began to dig in the red clay in one of the flowerbeds.

"What have you found?" asked Dennis in excitement. He helped Gnasher dig until at last they found...

"An old bone!" exclaimed Dennis. "HUMPH! We're looking for treasure, Gnasher!"

Dennis and Gnasher wandered all over the garden, digging holes in the flowerbeds and searching for treasure. They found a few more bones, a broken watch, fifteen pennies and a hedgehog having a late-night stroll, but no treasure.

As they were starting another hole, it started to rain. Soon they were happily plastered in thick, red mud. Then they heard a noise. It sounded like a key turning in a lock.

"Someone's coming out of the back door!" whispered Dennis. "Hide!"

They dived behind a bush and saw a torch bobbing across the garden towards them. As it passed them, they saw that it was carried by Mr Mulch! Mrs Mulch was close behind him, wearing a long black dressing gown that flapped in the wind.

"Come on,"
whispered Dennis. He and Gnasher
followed the Mulches across the
garden and past the stone wall.
When Dennis peered around the
corner, he saw a very strange sight
indeed. Behind the wall was a huge
cage, and it was full of bats!

"Weird-looking bats!"
said Dennis.
They weren't black like normal
bats. They were covered in white
splodges!
"You are a genius!" Mr Mulch
was saying to his wife. "What a
wonderful idea! To cross bats with
magpies!"

Mrs Mulch rubbed her hands together. "With the magpie's love for shiny things, our magbats will be able to steal things in the dark!" she cackled. "We'll be rich. RICH!"

"Bonkers," Dennis whispered, shaking his head.

"When will they be ready to steal for us?" asked Mr Mulch.

"We have to train them first," said Mrs Mulch. "And the best time for training magbats is at night!"

Gnasher was furious. He couldn't keep quiet any longer.

"GRRRRROOWWWWLLL!" he rumbled, stepping out from behind the wall. The Mulches whirled around. Gnasher bared his teeth and stuck all his fur on end. Mr Mulch went white and Mrs Mulch screamed.

"It's the Hound of the Moor!"

they shouted together. Gnasher's teeth were still luminous from the glow-in-the-dark sweets and his fur was red with mud!

Mr and Mrs Mulch dropped the torch and ran for the hostel, but in the dark they didn't see that Gnasher and Dennis had been digging.

" A A R R G G H H ! " yelled Mr Mulch as he stumbled into a flowerbed.

"EEEK!" squealed Mrs Mulch as she landed headfirst in a hole.

"Har har," sniggered Dennis, as he opened the cage. "Serves 'em right!"

The magbats swarmed out of the cage and flapped gratefully around Gnasher and Dennis, squeaking loudly. Gnasher howled "Don't mention it!" as lights started to go on all over the hostel.

Curtains were flung open and faces appeared at all the windows. They saw a terrifying sight! Mr and Mrs Mulch were upside down in the flowerbeds and there was a muddy boy-shaped monster leaping around the garden. Worst of all, the red Hound of the Moor was standing right outside the hostel, howling and baring his terrible glowing fangs! He was surrounded by a swarm of black-and-white bats that looked ready to attack – and there was a family in the tents nearby!

Screams came from every window in the hostel. Men fainted and women hid under the beds. No one noticed Dad peering out of his tent. No one saw him grab Dennis and Gnasher. No one spotted Dennis and his family racing back up the road to their car.

Dad turned the key in the ignition and let out a sigh of relief as the car started up. Mum wiped beads of sweat from her forehead. Dennis and Gnasher stared out of the back window at the hostel. They could see the swarm of magbats flying away and a stream of people running out of the hotel in panic.

"The Hound has eaten an entire family!" screamed one woman.

"Then it vanished into thin air!" shouted a man.

Dennis chuckled and grinned at Gnasher.

"That was one of the best menaces of all time!" he chortled. "We found some treasure, freed the magbats and started a legend! But you know what was best of all?"

Gnasher shrugged and Dennis gave a big wink.

"We showed Dad that fresh air isn't so good for you after all!"

More Bumper  fun...

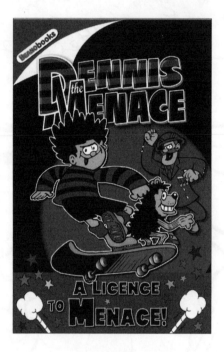

... make sure you've got them all!

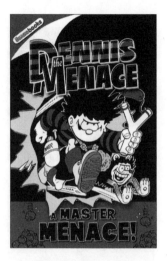

£3.99 1-84539-098-9

£3.99 1-84539-095-4

Follow the master of
menacing through a maze
of mischief and mayhem.

Grown-ups and softies
beware – Dennis is on
a mission to menace!

More Bumper fun...

£3.99 1-84539-097-0

£3.99 1-84539-096-2

Everyone knows a menace
somewhere... Now read
about the greatest
menace ever!

Dennis is back!
Join the mighty menace
as he creates more
crazy chaos!

... make sure you've got them all!

£3.99 1-84539-202-7   £3.99 1-84539-203-5

NEW to the Meadowside junior fiction range!

Minnie the Minx crashes in with these two great new titles
to keep her Beano buddy Dennis company.

Written by RACHEL ELLIOT

Illustrated by BARRIE APPLEBY

published under licence by

meadowside
CHILDREN'S BOOKS
185 Fleet Street, London, EC4A 2HS

10 9 8 7 6 5 4 3 2